THE YETI FILES

Monsters on the Run

KEVIN SHERRY

To my parents—thanks for all the art lessons.

Library of Congress Cataloging-in-Publication Data

Sherry, Kevin, author, illustrator.
  Monsters on the run / Kevin Sherry.
    pages cm. — (The Yeti files ; 2)
  Summary: Yeti Blizz Richards and his gang of cryptids set out to find a friend for Vanessa, the Loch Ness monster, even though it means traveling back in time to the dangerous age of the Cretaceous looking for plesiosaurs—unfortunately Vanessa proves to be rather timid about meeting other dinosaurs.
  ISBN 978-0-545-55619-4
1. Yeti—Juvenile fiction. 2. Loch Ness monster—Juvenile fiction. 3. Dinosaurs—Juvenile fiction. 4. Time travel—Juvenile fiction. 5. Friendship—Juvenile fiction. [1. Yeti—Fiction. 2. Loch Ness monster—Fiction. 3. Dinosaurs—Fiction. 4. Time travel—Fiction 5. Friendship—Fiction. 6. Humorous stories.] I. Title.
  PZ7.S549Mo 2015
  813.6—dc23
  [Fic]

                            2014049338

10 9 8 7 6 5 4 3 2 1   15 16 17 18 19

Printed in the U.S.A. 23
First edition, October 2015

Book design by Carol Ly

THE YETI FILES

Monsters on the Run

KEVIN SHERRY

Scholastic Press / New York

Thanks to Teresa Kietlinski, R. M. O'Brien, Ryan Patterson, Rachel Valsing, Dalen Beran, Jordan Card, Lisa Krause, Ed Schrader, Dan Deacon, Lizz King, and James Petz.

Chapter 1:
A GOOD LESSON

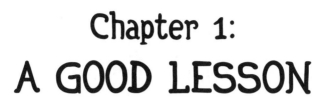

There's nothing better than playing with your pals.

Frank, Noodles...
fetch!

We'll fix it later. Right now, everyone come inside. Cousin Brian and I want to show you an important game.

Strength,
money,
and luck
can only get
you so far in life.

We cryptids
have to **use**
our brains
to protect
ourselves.

Brian and I will take turns drawing creatures we think are the **greatest**, the **mightiest**, and the **most powerful** around.

The most epic monster wins.

There are only two rules: **start small** and **admit defeat** if you've been beaten.

Okay, let's begin!

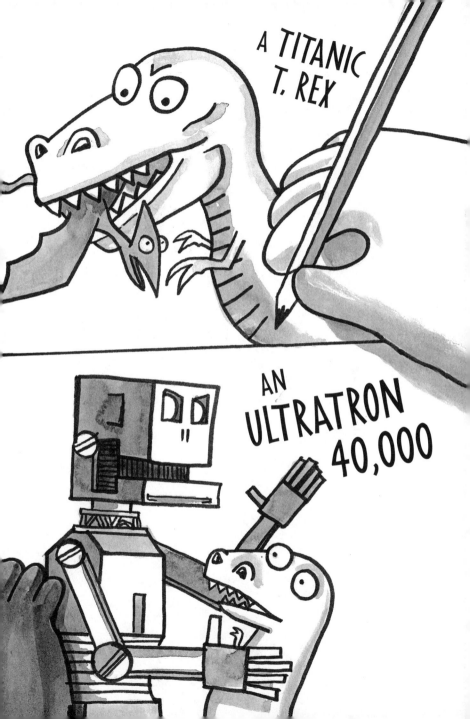

I summon Ulmog, THE ALL-SEEING, ALL-KNOWING, TENTACLED BEAST FROM BEYOND!

You got me! **A cute kitty always wins.**
It can melt the heart of even the most awful beasts.

Dear Blizz,

I'm lonely. I've got no one to talk to but frogs. If I can't find someone like me, I may have to leave Loch Ness.

Yours,
Vanessa

We have to help Nessie. She can't leave Loch Ness. That lake is her home. And it keeps her hidden.

Gang, it's time for a trip to Scotland.

CRYPTOTRON

DINNER ALONE

NO ONE LIKES MY TWEETS

#MELANCHOLY

I'll call Jack Saturday. Hopefully, he can give us a lift.

RING! RING!

ARENA

Extra!
Extra!

Can Jack
bring home
a win?

19

Well, hello. I'm Jack Saturday and I'm just about to win a very complicated game called the Rings of Alicornia. **Let me explain the rules.** But put your goggles on. Safety first!

Each team gets 10 rings:
9 silver and 1 gold. Players try to
toss their silver rings on the opposing
team's trees. To win, you must steal the
other team's gold ring and land it on the
Great Golden Spike, which I am just about to do.

Now, shhhh! I need to concentrate.

Chapter 3:
LONELY IN LOCH NESS

Ugh! Jack isn't picking up. How are we going to get to Scotland?

OOO
YES (TUBE) CUTE PIT BULL

Pump up your tires and slap on some bike shorts.

Wahoo!

If we can help her find **another creature like her,** maybe she'll be less lonely.

And we all know a happy cryptid is a hidden cryptid. We wouldn't want anyone to spot Nessie and discover her secrets, would we?

ENGLISH CHANNEL

FRANCE

27

SEAWEED FOR MILES

TWO CREEPING CATFISH

SUMMER SCHOOL OF FISH

That's all there is . . .

BORING OLD DUDES

29

As you can see, Blizz, **everyone here has someone.** Everyone has a perfect partner, playmate, and pal.

Everyone but me.

I've been doing some reading.

I think you are a plesiosaur.
But the last plesiosaur lived
65 million years ago!

Hey! That
looks like me!

His name is Tobin Clover, and he lives just across the water in Ireland. His pot-of-gold can do this neat little trick . . .

34

Chapter 4:
TOBIN'S MAGIC TRICK

Alex!

Hey, Tobin!

This is my boss, Blizz Richards, expert cryptozoologist. We have a tricky case that you may be able to help with.
Can we come inside?

FERGUS
THE CAT

HAT RACK

RESEARCH DEPARTMENT
SUPERCOMPUTER

Here's the situation.

Nessie wants to find others like her. Our plan is to travel 65 million years back in time.

Well, actually, I know a little
something about Vanessa—

Wait, wait, wait!
That's where you come in.
Alexander told us that
you have special . . . skills.

But don't you want
to know about . . .

First, I have to think a happy thought.

For me, that means thinking about my cat, Fergus. He always makes me smile. He makes me sneeze, too, but right now I'm focusing on happier things.

And that makes a rainbow appear.

Next, I grab the strands of the rainbow and separate them, picking out two colors to combine.

41

By linking the strands in new combinations, I can travel to different places and times.

Like present-day New York or long-ago Easter Island.

I go back in time to right before a disaster is about to strike.

And I beam these objects to safety before they can be destroyed.

POOF!

45

It took a few tries for Tobin to get them where they wanted to go . . .

Chapter 5:
PREHISTORIC PROBLEMS

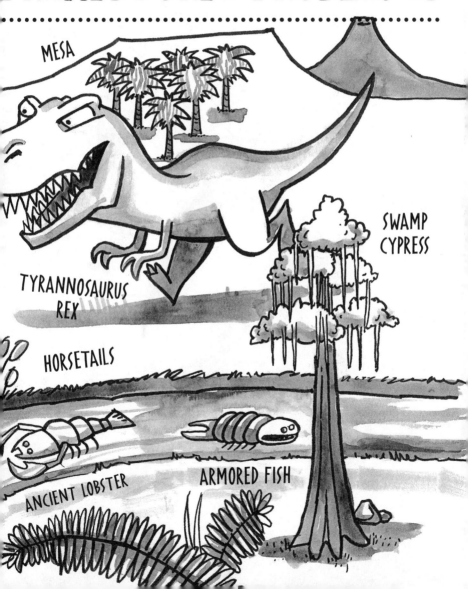

MESA

SWAMP CYPRESS

TYRANNOSAURUS REX

HORSETAILS

ANCIENT LOBSTER

ARMORED FISH

The team darted away on Nessie's back...

Don't get separated, guys!

. . . and immediately got **separated!**

They landed in five different spots.

SEA

CLIFFS

Ouch!

54

Chapter 6:
BLIZZ ON THE CASE

Meanwhile, Blizz searched for a plesiosaur to pair up with Nessie.

I'm looking for a dinosaur.

HADROSAUR

He's pretty huge. Like this.

ANKYLOSAURUS

I like to eat jellyfish.

PROTOSTEGA

COELACANTH

Actually, you are on the right track.

Chapter 7:
A DANGEROUS LAND

But Nessie wasn't finding prehistoric waters nearly so friendly.

Who are these monsters?

I have got to get out of here!

SCRUBLAND

HIGH MOUNTAINS

DRY DESERT

STEEP CLIFFS

Over here!

Meanwhile, Tobin had finally found someone who'd listen to him.

I was sightseeing in Pisa, Italy, when I saw some workers building a bell tower. It began to sink on one side. They wanted to fix it, but I told them it had character.

I like traveling back to ancient Alexandria, to read the scrolls in the library of knowledge. I once discovered a great old recipe for grape soda.

You know what the Sphinx looks like, right? Well, it actually used to have a nose! It fell off during an earthquake and I rescued it. I'm waiting for the right time to give it back.

And you've seen those sculptures on Easter Island? Well, I shouldn't say this, but they are actually hat racks for some other cryptids . . . the giants.

Chapter 8½:
FRIENDS IN NEED

Protoceratops to the rescue!

Chapter 9:
DANGER IN THE DEEP

Nessie was finally making friends, too...

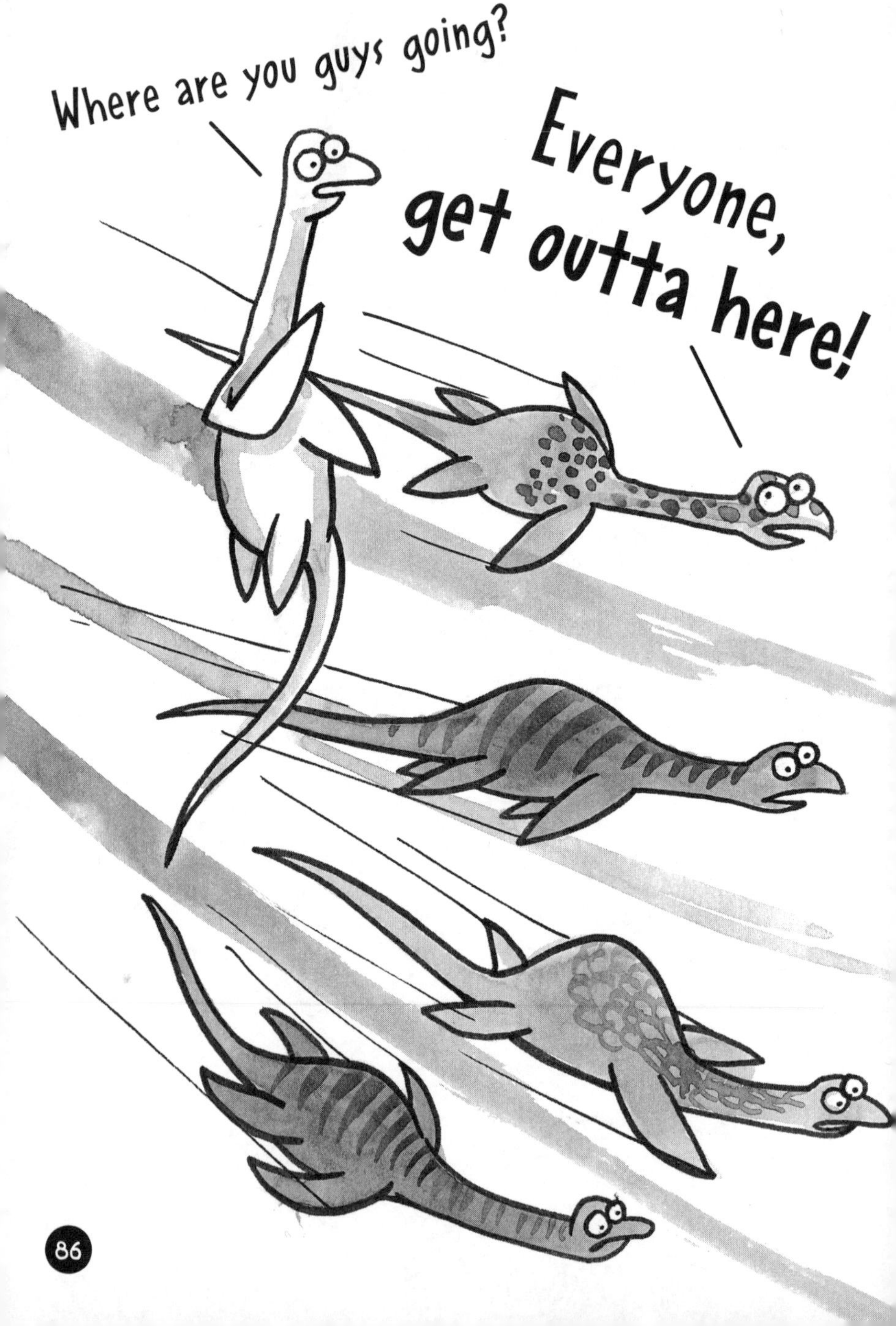
Where are you guys going?
Everyone, get outta here!

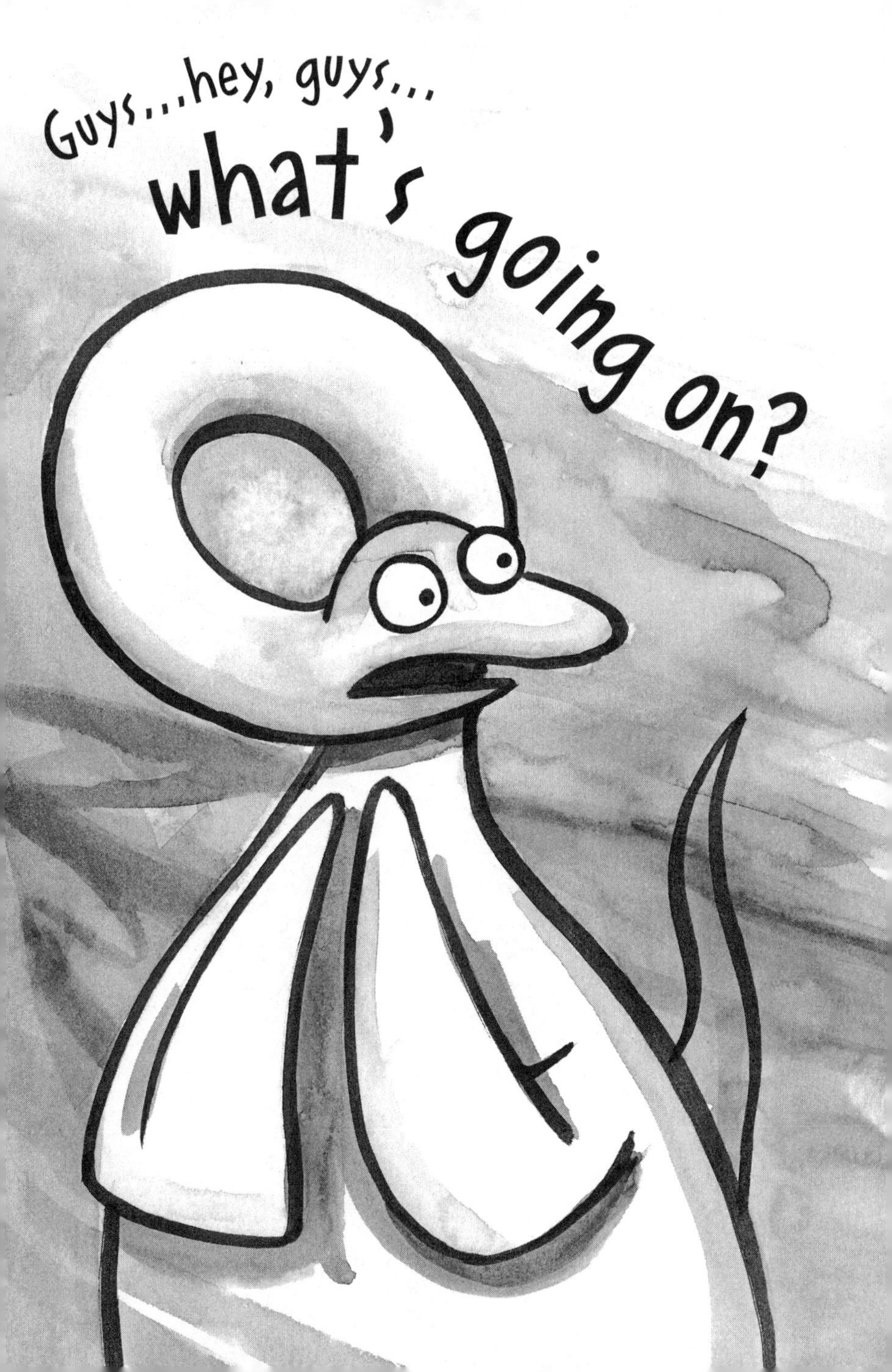
Guys...hey, guys...
what's going on?

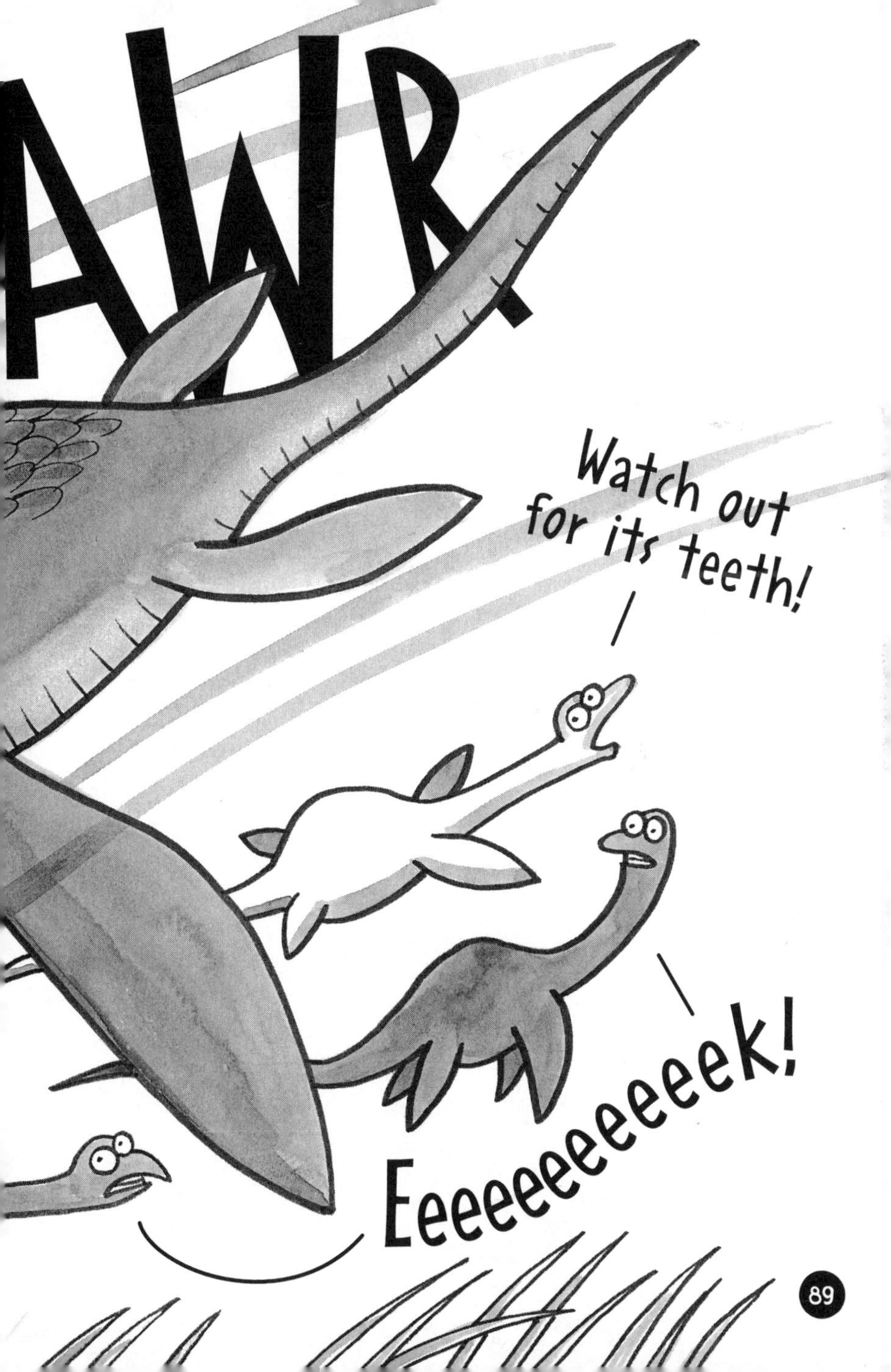
AWR
Watch out for its teeth!
Eeeeeeeeeeek!

Nessie hightailed it out of the lake.

Hey, Blizz, we've got to get out of here.

It's too scary,

I want to go back home.

91

Now that I know what it's like for others like me, my life in the future doesn't seem so bad.

Plus, I'm not really alone after all.

I have friends so good they'll travel 65 million years back in time and risk their lives just to help me.

Great!
Now we just have to find Tobin and the rest of the team.

Who is going to make me? You?
I'm the greatest, mightiest,
most powerful
creature around!
SCRIBBLE

Chapter 10:
BACK TO THE FUTURE

Gunthar!
You saved us!

And you were paying
attention to our image
scrimmage lesson.

Tobin! Noodles! You found us? But how?

Let's just say this story could also be called *The Yeti Files 2: Loudest Cryptids of All Time.*

POOF!

Chapter 11:
TOBIN TELLS THE TRUTH

Blizz, that was terribly dangerous, absolutely reckless, and totally **fun** and **rewarding!**

I better be
going now.

But if you don't mind,
Noodles is going to
stay here with me.
He's a great listener.

There is **another sea monster like you, Vanessa.**

And he lives with my cousin here in the present.

Here's a file
I put together
for you.

And met **Chester** the Chesapeake Bay monster, also known as Chessie.

Oh, my goodness!

Chapter 12:
NEW SURPRISES

Great job, team. I'm going to surf the Internet. There's some lasagna in the fridge if you're hungry.

Hey, Alexander,
I know how you like to collect stuff, sooo . . .
I got you a souvenir from our trip!
Guess we're going to find out!
Oh, no! What is it?

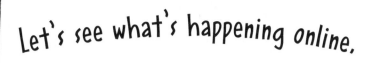

Let's see what's happening online.

CRYPTOTRON

BLIZZ RICHARDS:
GOTTA CATCH UP ON MY TV

CHUPACABRA:
#GOATSSUCKER4LIFE

RAT KING:
THESE RAVIOLI, FUGEDABOUTIT

MOTH MAN:
BZZ BZZZT BUZZERT

CHESSIE:
I THINK I'M IN LOVE

ZOMBIE:
UUUUNG UUNG

We gotta take care of that.
But first, let's call Jack!

Maybe his schedule has finally cleared up enough that he can help us get where we're needed. Our legs can't handle another bike ride, especially under water!

Congratulations to
Jack Saturday, MVP!
Blizz, can I call you back?
Yay!
Yay!
THE END!

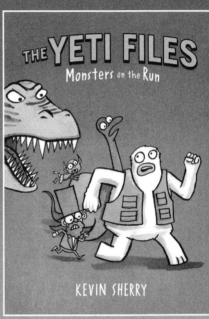